natalie russell

Lost for Words

MACMILLAN CHILDREN'S BOOKS

Tapir had some pencils
and a nice new notebook.

But he didn't know
what to write.

He stared at the clean page and
tried to think of something. Anything!
But nothing popped into his head.
It felt empty, just like his page.

Tapir's friends could write words easily,
about things that meant a lot to them.

Giraffe was writing a poem about his favourite tree.
He chewed its leaves as he wrote . . .

You are tall and thin, my perfect tree.
You reach so high, just like me!
Your leaves so juicy and good to chew,
Oh precious tree, I do love you.

Giraffe had a way with words.

Hippo was in his muddy pool,
writing an exciting story . . .

Once upon a time there lived a very handsome hippo. One day, while dozing in the pool, he heard a bird cry for help. What a disaster! She was stuck in the mud! The very handsome hippo swam bravely to her rescue. "My hero," chirped Bird. Thank goodness the handsome hippo was an excellent swimmer.

THE END

He always knew how to begin a story and how it would end. Hippo was very clever.

Flamingo was composing
a song about the sun.
She hummed softly as
she wrote . . .

When the sun shines brightly in the sky,
I feel so happy, I want to fly!
I stretch my neck and fluff my feathers.
For me, sunshine is the best of weathers.
But when the clouds come and then the rain,
My long long legs become cold again!

Her song was so perfect it brought a tear to Tapir's eye.

I must be doing something wrong, thought Tapir.

So he tried humming,

and wallowing.

He even chewed on
some juicy leaves.

But no words came.
And the harder he tried
the crosser he felt.

"It's not fair!" said Tapir.

"Don't worry," said his friends. "You'll think of something."

But Tapir wasn't so sure,
and he walked away . . .

. . . far away, to a quiet place on top of the hill.
And there Tapir looked out at the beautiful view,
and began to think.

Then, very carefully, he opened his notebook and unpacked his pencils.

And without a word he drew the sun,
big and round, right at the top of his page.
A bright sun especially for Flamingo.

Under the sun Tapir drew the river,
long and winding, down to the pool
where Hippo liked to play.

He added plenty of mud
to keep Hippo happy.

Next to Hippo's pool he drew a tall tree. Tapir covered it in fresh green leaves because he knew Giraffe would like it that way.

When Tapir had finished he looked proudly at what he'd drawn.

But there was something missing . . .

. . . three friends so important that
they needed a page all of their own!

6

Tapir rushed back to show his friends what he'd drawn.

"How wonderful you are!" said Giraffe.
"You draw so well," said Hippo.
"It's beautiful," whispered Flamingo,
wiping a tear from her eye.

Tapir didn't need words after all. Not one!
His colourful drawings said everything he wanted to say.

And they said it perfectly.